日 落 時 候 想 唱 歌

The Desire to Sing after Sunset
paintings and poems by Ami

阿米

1980年次，台灣女詩人和畫家。
2011年第一本詩集《要歌要舞要學狼》入選台灣文學獎金典獎。
同年舉辦她的第一個畫展。
2012年出版第一本長篇小說《慾望之閣》。
2012年與黑眼睛跨劇團合作，擔任音樂劇作詞人。
《日落時候想唱歌》收錄2009至2013年間的畫作。
2013年出版與潘家欣往來的詩歌書信詩集《她是青銅器我是琉璃》。
2013年策展「公寓秀－請按電鈴」，邀請12位年輕與壯年詩人在公寓內展出私物件,包括畫作,手稿,日記,襪子,t - shirt......並連續舉辦「衛生紙沙龍」包括戲劇表演與講座。
2009年由鴻鴻挖掘,自《衛生紙+》創刊以來,成為其重要詩人之一。

Ami

(1980-) is a Taiwanese poet and painter.
Her first volume *To Sing, To Dance, To Be A Wolf* was nominated for the prestigious Taiwan Literature Award in 2011.
In the same year, her first exhibition of paintings opened.
Her first full - length novel *The Light in the Attic* was published in 2012.
Also in 2012, she worked as a librettist with the Dark Eyes performance lab.
The Desire to Sing after Sunset selects her paintings from 2009－2012.
She is Bronze, I'm Liuli... a poetic exchange with Chia - Hsin Pan in the form of letters appeared in 2013.
Also in 2013, Ami invited twelve poets of differing ages to exhibit their personal belongings (paintings, scripts, diaries, socks, t - shirts, etc) in *The Flat Show - Please Ring the Doorbell*.
Her "Off the Roll Poetry Salon" includes performance art and seminars.
Ami was discovered by Hung Hung in 2009. She has been one of the most significant poets since Off The Roll was founded.

范秀明

巴西出生台灣長大，輔大英語系畢業，英國翻譯口譯碩士。現居巴西，靠一張嘴、二隻手、三種語言吃飯。

Ingrid Fan was born in Brazil, where she spent her childhood before returning to her cultural roots in Taiwan. She has a BA in English from Fu Jen University and an MA in Translation and Interpreting from the University of Salford, UK. She likes to think she is living proof that even if translations cannot be beautiful and remain faithful, translators can.

Matt Bryden

英國貝克漢出生長大。EFL老師一職帶領他到托斯坎尼、捷克和波蘭。他的詩冊 Night Porter 贏得2010年 Templar Pamphlet and Collection 獎。他的作品在英國廣泛出版，翻譯作品也出現於Modern Poetry in Translation。他第一本詩集 Boxing the Compass 將於Templar 出版。

Born and raised in Beckenham, Matt Bryden is an EFL teacher whose work has taken him to Tuscany, the Czech Republic and Poland. His pamphlet *Night Porter* was a winner of the Templar Pamphlet and Collection award 2010. His work is widely published in the UK, and his translations have appeared in *Modern Poetry in Translation*. His first collection *Boxing the Compass* appeared in 2013.

魔幻的邊界
盛正德

採擷三個月藍天的藍
流盡體內鮮紅的血
整季春雨後的綠
小喇叭吹奏出最高亢的黃
這樣的顏料都嫌不足
因為妳窺見的是
人們噤聲止步的邊境
　　必須
以高分貝的囈語　高彩度的色彩
才勉可描述　之後沉默闇然

Sightlines
Sheng Zheng De

Blue plucked from three months' skies
Red bled from the body
Green after a season of spring rain
Yellow played by a trumpet

Each colour is insufficient –
your glimpse of the border that is kept
requires

a high decibel rave, saturated colours
to approach its essence;
and then the silence and darkness.

當火焰投射出長長的黑暗
文/潘家欣

第一次讀阿米的詩，我就被震動了，文字閃亮，寓意深刻。能夠在字裡行間綻放光彩的
年輕詩人很多，而能夠真正撼動靈魂的，卻永遠少之又少，阿米便是其中一位。而後，
我與阿米結識，又見到了她的畫，更加驚豔。

阿米長時間受精神分裂症所苦，在英國唸書期間發作，在機場、警察局、陌生街道中迷
走。恐怖蠱影化成真實夢境，藥劑越吃越重，諮商師建議阿米可以通過藝術創作的方式
療癒自己，於是阿米開始寫詩，也斷續的寫小說，去畫室學著畫自己，捉捕糾纏不去的
執妄群像，命之現形，化成畫布上的筆觸與色彩。這些畫作有如鑽石耀眼，是她從地獄
深淵中一步一步爬出來的拖痕，是重生血路上開出來的一些曼陀羅花。

你可以在這本書的分輯中，看見阿米最憂鬱狂亂時期的漂流掙扎。可以看見她在病中渴
望愛，也溫柔的愛著那個戴帽的男子。最後，你可以看見她以一個柔弱之軀，如何成為
有翼的天使。

阿米的詩與畫，有人會稱之為靈光一現的天才，阿米也深為此苦惱過，擔心自己的作品
只是偶然的奇蹟。但是與阿米認識這幾年來，我深知這一切並非奇蹟或是天才，而是阿
米用十年患病的人生，釀出了一杯苦冽的藥酒，喝下去，她才有力氣做下一階段的夢。
當火焰投射出長長的黑暗，不要害怕深不見底的無眠，走進去吧，並且走向更遠更遠
處，全然輕盈的甦醒。

人生所失去的時間、空間、記憶，是否會以同等重量的創作回到身邊？傷痛又是否真能
被時間撫慰？

藝術是否真能拯救靈魂？

且看這一本《日落時候想唱歌》，一起親眼見證生命中的火焰，愛，死亡與重生。

When Fire Throws Long Shadows
By Chia-Hsin Pan

When I first read Ami's poems I was deeply moved. They are vivid and profound. Many young people's words shine, but few can truly touch souls. Ami is one of those few. Meeting Ami in person, and then seeing her paintings, I was moved still further.

Ami's schizophrenia first became apparent while she was studying in the UK. At the airport, in a police station and on the streets of London she lost her sense of reality. Dreadful hallucinations became waking dreams and her medication had to be increased.

Her therapist suggested that she heal herself through creation, and so she started to write poems, and novels intermittently. She also taught herself to paint, capturing some of the haunting illusions and transforming them into brush-strokes and colours on the canvas. These paintings dazzle like diamonds, and are the scars of her dragging herself from the brink of the abyss. They are the thorned roses growing along the bloody road to rebirth.

In this book, we witness Ami's struggle through the most frenzied and introspective period of her life. We can see her thirst for love during her sickness, and her tender love for the 'man with hat.' In the end, we see how she transformed herself from a frail body into an angel with wings.

Some people regard Ami's poems and paintings as a gift but briefly bestowed on her. In this regard, Ami fears that her work is only a fortuitous event. But in the years I've known her I have come to understand that it is neither a miracle nor fleeting genius. It is a strong and bitter liquor, distilled from many years of illness.

Only by drinking it does she possess the strength to progress to her next dream. When the fire throws long shadows, do not fear the abyss, just plunge into it and go deeper – and wake up reinvigorated.

Can one reclaim in art what one has lost in life?

Or will wounds draw themselves closed in time?

Can art truly save the soul?

Read *The Desire to Sing after Sunset.* Witness with your own eyes the fire, love, death and rebirth.

Death and Fire

The Man with Hat

Madness is Real

✝ Death

and

Fire

葉青

我也抽很多菸
一天吃十顆
我知道像死一樣地逃進睡眠
我憂鬱、瘋狂而且發胖
小你一歲
我知道精神科等待的時光會看見什麼樣的白
長年無業
而且我寫詩

如何跟一次都沒死過的人討論死亡 [1]
我們可以一起研究自殺的方法
或者靠著背活下來
只差一點點
親愛的葉青
只要再老一點
我們就能活成怕死的人

我知道詩停在這邊最好
但這對大家而言太痛苦
我願意多寫一行
再一行
因為活下去需要一點希望

---

[1] 葉青與我同為衛生紙詩人，32歲自殺，身後留下兩本詩集，此為葉青〈我們——致老王〉詩句

Yeh Ching

I too smoke a lot,
take ten pills a day.
I know how to escape into my sleep like
                                        the dead.
I am depressed, insane and fat.
one year younger than you.
I know the kind of white I'll see while
                    waiting at the psychiatrist's.
Unemployed for years
and I write poems.

How to discuss death with someone who
                    has not died once?[1]
We could study suicide methods together
or survive with each other's support.
Almost.
Dear Yeh Ching,
just a bit older,
we could live as people afraid of death.

I know the poem had better end here
but it is too painful for everybody.
I am willing to write one more line,
one more line,
because to live needs a little hope.

---

[1] Yeh Ching, a fellow *Off the Roll* poet, committed suicide at 32 leaving two collections behind her. 'How to...' is a reference to her poem 'From Us to Old Wang'

這麼多年了，在箱子和梅雨　　　　Years in the box, the plum rain
我可以活　　　　　　　　　　　　I could take it

回到一個人居住的房間　　　　　　Move back to my single room
剪斷繩索　　　　　　　　　　　　cut my ties

冷酷嚴峻的海岸地帶　　　　　　　Coastline ruthless and grim,
蛇一般惡毒的斷崖　　　　　　　　cliffs venomous as serpents,
生日沒有願望　　　　　　　　　　prospectless birthdays

這一切不能只是消失　　　　　　　None of these can just vanish
非要轉化成藝術　　　　　　　　　but must be transformed into art
否則此心永不復活　　　　　　　　should the heart revive

另一個房間
它吞
所有的業障
沒有解藥、亦沒有日出
不需要治療，亦不曾疼
會畫星星的人
住下來

The other room strikes
all karma from the chart

Asks not antidote, sunrise
therapy or pain

The star painter stays

你有一雙受苦的眼睛
我不敢多看，看了會想哭
——友人

我有一雙受苦的眼睛
已不想細數一生的不幸
出版詩集，還給老天
讓傷痕自我眼底發芽

你不敢多看
除了一眼
沒有更多
看了一眼便是心痛了

看了會想哭
那便一起到一棵大樹下約會
交換彼此的年輪
然後砍掉
好像沒有來過

Your eyes have known pain.
I daren't look, or I'll cry
– dear friend.

Mine, too. I no longer want
to count my life's miseries,
publish poetry and return them to God,
let the spring appear in my eyes.

You hardly dare look –

just a glimpse
no more,
even a glimpse hurts.

Since looking makes you cry,
let's make a date under a large tree
exchange annual rings
then cut it down
as if we'd never been there.

生命像一條尼龍繩索
圈繞著脖子

鬆鬆的時候
我尖叫
活著真好

束起的時候
我害怕
殺死自己的慾望

反覆之間
我們如狗吐著舌頭

這一天要去摩天輪
還是臥軌

Life is like a nylon rope
around my neck

When it is loose
I cry -
being alive is good

When it is tight
I fear the desire
to kill myself

Again and again
we are like dogs panting

On this day,
shall I take a ride on a Ferris Wheel
or take my life on the railway tracks?

未完成的畫布
石頭、橋、流水⋯
這一筆越來越逼真

Each brushstroke
a little more vivid,
river, rock, bridge...

有人呼喚你
你一回頭，才驚覺
這哭
這苦
這一生越來越抽象

At your name, you turn:
a sea of mourners, weeping,
pained—increasingly surreal

The Man with Hat

他們只是玩具

在你的國
我何嘗不是一個小兵

只是這河

讀過了詩
我也變成土做的

一點春雨
便化成泥

They are just toys

In your kingdom
Aren't I just a foot soldier?

Before me this river -

After reading poems
I have turned into soil

Spring rain falls on me -
And I muddy

讓一切腐朽

蘋果變黃
老黃狗貪睡
蠟燭燒到了世界的盡頭

花朵隨著四季輪迴
祖母的肉身化成土壤
老舊的屋舍和社區老樹在政客的舌尖消失

唯有不經意與你路過婚紗街的午后
仍然是一半斜陽，一半天真

Let them all rot

An apple browns
An old dog drowses
A candle burns till the end of the world

Flowers reincarnate through the seasons
Grandmother's flesh becomes dirt
Clapped - out houses and old trees disappear through
politicians' tongues

Only this afternoon, we passed through a street
of wedding dress shops, a little light still to the day, half innocent

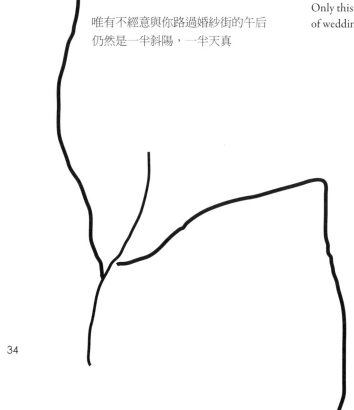

因為愛你
我成了最佳的喜劇演員

Loving you
Made me the best comic actress

不要打開　　　Do not open it
光進來　　　　Once the light comes in
我就不見了　　I will vanish

我是花
想打開花瓣
因為受夠了，黑色之書
因為前面所吃的苦

I am a flower
That wants to bloom
Because of the pain I suffered
And too much gloom

陽光潑在我的腳下
提醒我黑夜過去了

但是，醒來之後
要去哪兒？

我化妝
穿新衣
準備出門

最遠走到巷子口
彷彿就已經碰到了世界的盡頭

Sunlight at my feet
reminds me night has passed.

But, where to
after waking up

all set,
my face on,
in new clothes?

The furthest I can go is the end of this alley,
the end of the world.

Madness

is

Real

一開始只是吞藥
後來發現
火車、火箭、火藥
我都能吞嚥下去

吞行星、吞礦脈、吞月亮……
吞一切之黑暗苦難
吞一支筆所寫不出來的
淚痕

In the beginning, it was only meds I swallowed
but then I realized –
trains, rockets, gunpowder,

I could swallow them, too.

Planet, lode, moon,
I could swallow all the dark miseries,
swallow the tear-stains

which a pen can't write.

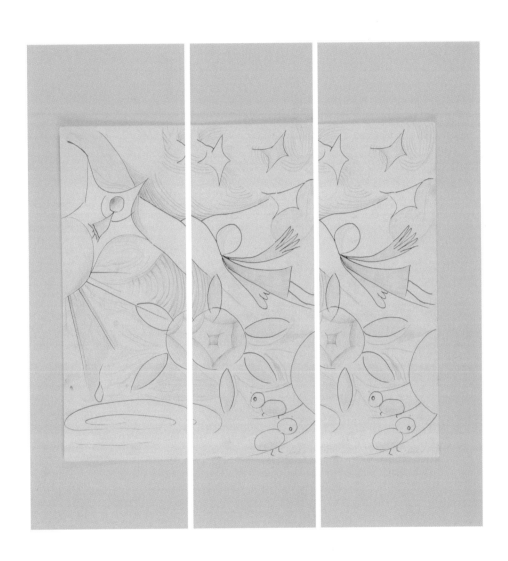

吃過苦的人
來唷
來打拳擊
重重倒地
不怕
用爬的我也曾爬過

趴在河底，生命靜止不動
病房的人，藥吃太多
人人像一顆緩慢的鐘

我已經不恨冬天
也不恨下雨
痂像美麗刺青，但不願意重來

You who have suffered
Come!
Come fight it out —

If you are knocked down
Do not fear
Crawl as I once did

On the bottom of the river, life stays still
In a hospice, there are too many drugs
The patients are wound like slack clocks

I no longer hate the winter
Nor the rain
A scar is a beautiful tattoo, but never again

一個瘋子是真實的

海洋沒有話要說

Madness is real

The ocean has nothing to say

整個夏天
流星不斷閃過
擦亮我的背、腰、臀……
最終是前額銀亮的犄角
於是又全黑

下一個夏天
我要到公園散步：
人、水鳥和風。
那又是另一個特技了

All summer
Meteors crossed the sky
Polished my back, haunches, rump...
And finally the silver horn on my forehead
But everything reverted to darkness

Next summer
I shall walk in the park
People, birds and wind
Another of my tricks

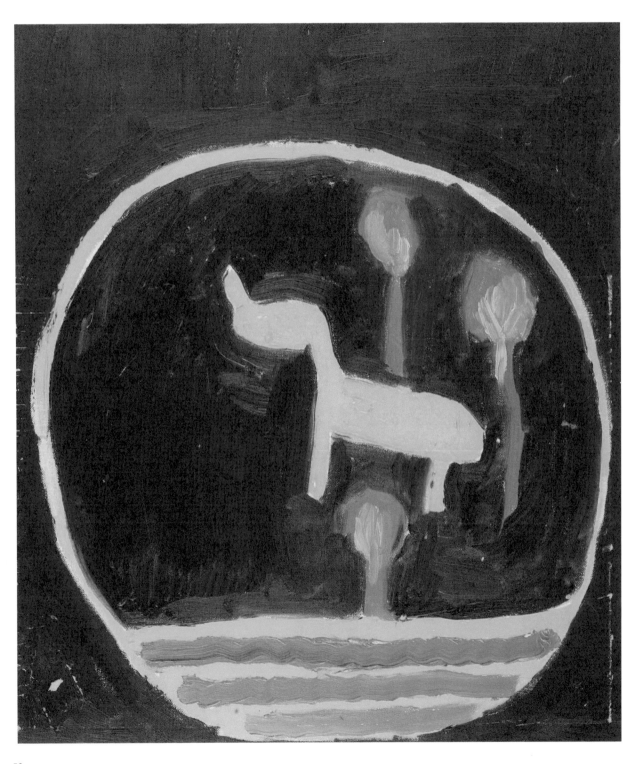

53

不要夢
不要黎明
不要天真

我要你爲我犯罪
撬開我的牡蠣
我要再一次落難

我們彼此驗傷
共用一個靜止的鏡頭

病發了，就餵彼此吃藥
睡醒了就去IKEA過日子

不養狗
不養貓
不養鳥
不養魚
不養孩子
甚至不創作

No dreams
No dawn
No innocence

I want you to commit a crime for me
Pry my oyster shell
I want to fall into misfortune again

We lick each other's wounds
Sharing a quiet camera shot

When sick, we feed each other drugs
When awake, we live in IKEA

No cats
No dogs
No birds
No fish
No kids
Not even creating

John

畢竟我是水象星座 很容易就濕了	A water sign I get wet easily

甜蜜轉眼痛苦 用詩的複眼去愛 痛苦 轉眼甜蜜	Blink, and love becomes pain See it poetically, Blink, becomes love again

我心底有一百隻飛鳥 你可以教我唱一首慢歌嗎？	Hundreds of birds fly in my heart Won't you teach me to sing a slow song?

John

He owns a youthful horn
Yet not this devilish loneliness

他是擁有青春犄角的獸
但他還未擁有我輩魔鬼的寂寞

大雨中
含一顆酸梅
我想你，但沒有你

In the pouring rain
A sour plum remains in my mouth
I miss you, only there is no you

Jolly

Singer

我看著你離開
整個夏天
留下一顆橘子
既不甜美
也無法消化

你所寫的詩
我都大聲朗讀
因此錯過了花季

我成不了牧園的歌者
也無法帶走你

After a whole summer
you left me
an orange
Neither sweet
nor digestible

I read your poems aloud
and so missed the flowering season

Neither pastureland vocalist
nor your fellow walker

渴望吮奶
我知道我缺乏

渴望妳如步入山頂上的教堂
渴望深夜被抱走
渴望退縮成一小顆種子
渴望最初的擁抱

渴望妳，用一隻雛鳥的眼睛
母親，一定是妳的強悍
使我成爲一個脆弱的表演者

或者一個渴望受控制的偶人
妳若剪斷麻繩
我將瓦解

母親，我將一飲而盡
妳愛裡頭的恨意

I long to breast feed,
know I'm lacking something -

for you to walk into the church
at the top of the mountain,
abduct me in the deep of the night;
for me to retreat to a seed;

for that first embrace
I long for you, with my nestling eyes.

Mother, it must be your ferocity
has made me a weak performer
or a puppet who longs to be controlled.

Cut the strings
and I collapse.

Mother, I'll drink up
the hate in your love.

我看見明天
路問著它的終點
秋千問風的起點
我沾滿塵土的鞋子沉默
我聽見媽媽的笑聲，雖然我不知道她在何處
新的一年來了；新的願望在狗的尾巴

I see tomorrow,
The street asks where it ends.
The swing asks the wind for a beginning,
My dusty shoes remain silent.
I hear my mother's laughter,
Though I don't know where she is;
New Year is coming, resolution at the dog's tail.

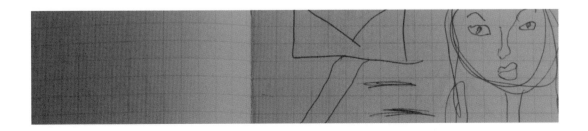

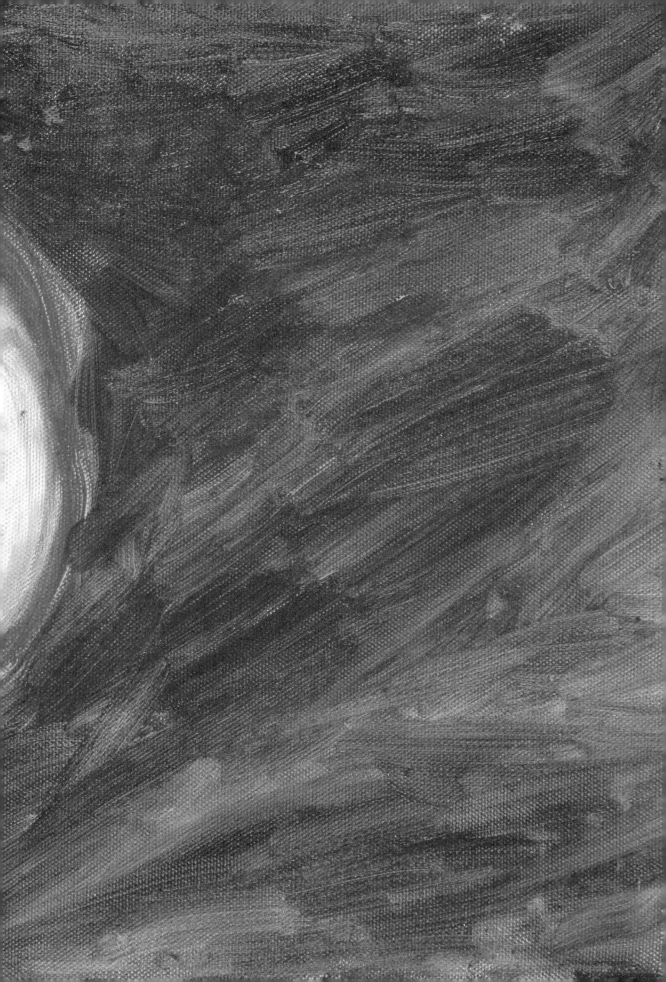

我知道你會爲一場陣雨感傷
我知道你和我一樣傾聽過雷鳴

厄運時你問：爲什麼是我？
幸福來臨時你問：爲什麼是我？

我知道這座吊橋的意義
你的眼淚
和你靈魂的歌聲
我都爲你守護

我知道你的母貓
臨死前交代你什麼
像你的母親
臨死前告訴你的

我知道安靜的果實
所能代表的喜悅
我知道你的吻
能抵達
多深

我知道痛苦能讓人謙虛
我知道黑暗之後光明不一定到來

我知道猴子棲息的夜晚
我知道蘋果熟透需要時間

我知道你抱著自己的孩子
我知道這一切已經足夠

I know you get sentimental over the rain,
I know you listen to the thunder like I do.

In misfortune you ask, 'Why me?'
In happiness, 'Why me?'

I know what this suspension bridge means,
your tears
and your soul's tune:
I defend them both for you.

I know your cat's
last words,
the same as
your mother's,

I know how significant is the joy
of the fruit of silence,
how deep

your kiss
reaches,

I know pain can humble a man,
I know light doesn't always come after dark.

I know the night the monkey rests in,
I know an apple needs time to ripen.

I know you hold your own baby.
I know all of this, and it is ample.

The world is meat — you're the tenderest part

陽光很漂亮，我看見漂亮卻感覺到一絲腐朽，花瓶可承受得了花的死亡？
小貓小狗天天幾公噸、幾公噸地安樂死，死有甚麼可怕。

這樣的光線下，怪手也是美麗的，拆除家園也是美麗的，所有殘酷都是詩興的
殺戮也是，只要天氣好，一切都是美麗的，壯麗的，而我們還有音樂、舞蹈、香
菸、美酒。

我們查農民曆，宜往北方走。

Sunshine is beautiful, I see its beauty but also a hint of decay. Can the vase bear the
flower's death? Every day, by the pound, cats and dogs are put to sleep. What is to be
feared of death? In such a light, bulldozers are pretty, demolishing houses pretty, all forms
of cruelty poetic - even killing, as long as the weather is good. Everything is pretty and
splendid. We still have music, dancing, cigarettes and wine. Sunshine is beautiful. I looked
it up in the Almanac, it's auspicious to go north.

Since you left, no clock wakes me

你的手穿過我的手，天空的雨，彼此吞沒，五月的你和山羊跳舞，陽光使你變成粉紅色，我想偷看你的ㄋㄟㄋㄟ

鬼月燒化一本詩集，亡靈月光下旋轉，他們安靜喜悅，左派、反核、反媒體壟斷，喜歡威化餅乾和洗手台又有一點小資情調

王爾德那痴情的夜鶯只會一首情詩，只會高音，玫瑰臉很紅，不要拒絕我和我的青春痘。你的情歌我都喜歡背誦，只是可否再慢一點，像一頂帽子吃掉一頭大象那樣的慢

我愛你的副歌和吊帶褲，但厭倦半夜和你爭吵。我知道你喜歡夏宇和她的一串風鈴，偶爾也讀我的詩，但不要相信房地產廣告，不要抄襲泰戈爾，否則我會覺得你淺薄，你是厚的厚的，相信我烤巧克力口味厚片土司很讚，大人口味的唷

Your hands in my hands, the rain engulfing us. You in May dancing with a goat, the sunshine making you pink. I want to steal a glimpse at your breasts, burn a poetry collection during Ghost Month. The ghosts dance in the moonlight–quiet, joyous, left-wing, anti-nuke. They love wafers and sinks and have slightly petit-bourgeois taste. Oscar Wilde's devoted nightingale knows only one love poem, can sing only in a high pitch. The rose's face is bright-red, don't turn me or my spots down. I like to recite all your love songs. Would you slow down a bit though–as slow as a hat eats an elephant. I love your chorus and overalls, but hate fighting with you in the middle of the night. I know you like Hsia Yu and her wind chimes. And sometimes you read my poems. However, don't trust the real estate ads or plagiarize Tagore or I'll think you shallow; when you are deep and believe that my baked chocolate toast is fantastic–its adult flavour.

Rabbit

Beam

Rabbit Beam

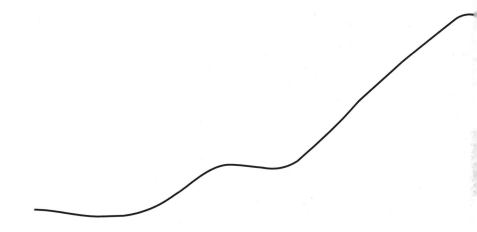

ere comes Rabbit Beam with his bag.

can dance with my bag. " Rabbit Beam feels like a drum.

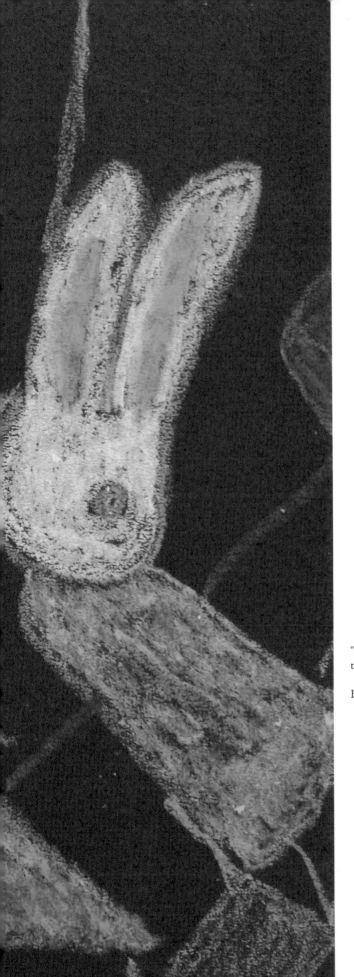

"For you it's only a bag, but it belongs to me," says Beam. "If you take it away, I will be bad." Beam's bag knows him the best.

Beam's always alone like a swing in the wind.

"Don't touch me!" cries Beam. "Don't take it from me." Beam is scared.
"Do they really understand us?" he wonders.

"Nobody likes a sad rabbit," Beam says to his bag. "You're my best friend."

"Am I a good rabbit? Shall we part? Do I look handsome with my bag?"

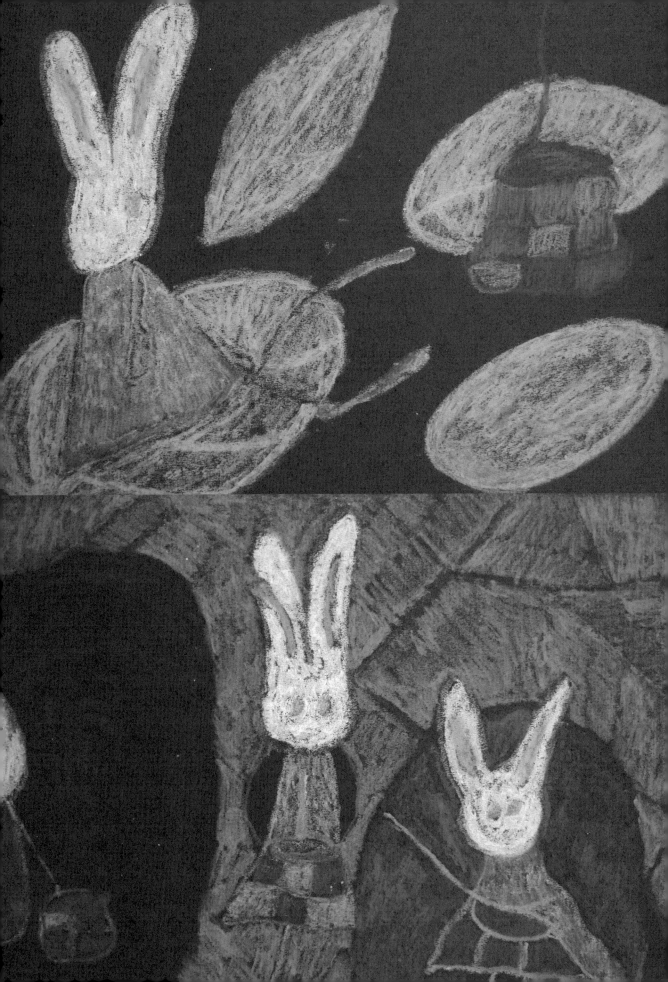

"If the wind blows, we move with it...
If the ocean sings, our hearts beat like drums...
As I read, I become a fish to hear raindrops in the river..."
Beam shares so many beautiful things with his bag.

But, he's not happy. Maybe he needs to put some carrots into his bag. Will he?

讀詩人42　PG1007

 日落時候想唱歌
　　　　　——阿米中英圖畫詩集

作　　者	阿　米
責任編輯	黃姣潔
圖文排版	陳發昀
封面設計	陳發昀
英　　譯	Matt Bryden、Ingrid Fan

出版策劃	釀出版
製作發行	秀威資訊科技股份有限公司
	114 台北市內湖區瑞光路76巷65號1樓
	電話：+886-2-2796-3638　傳真：+886-2-2796-1377
	服務信箱：service@showwe.com.tw
	http://www.showwe.com.tw
郵政劃撥	19563868　戶名：秀威資訊科技股份有限公司
展售門市	國家書店【松江門市】
	104 台北市中山區松江路209號1樓
	電話：+886-2-2518-0207　傳真：+886-2-2518-0778
網路訂購	秀威網路書店：http://www.bodbooks.com.tw
	國家網路書店：http://www.govbooks.com.tw
法律顧問	毛國樑　律師
總 經 銷	創智文化有限公司
	236 新北市土城區忠承路89號6樓
	電話：+886-2-2268-3489　傳真：+886-2-2269-6560
	博訊書網：http://www.booknews.com.tw

出版日期	2013年10月　BOD一版
定　　價	420元

Printed in Taiwan

國家圖書館出版品預行編目

日落時候想唱歌 / 阿米作. -- 一版. -- 臺北市：釀出版,
　2013.10
　　面；　　公分. -- (讀詩人 ; 42) (語言文學類 ;
PG1007)
　　中英對照
　　BOD版
　　ISBN 978-986-5871-62-8 (平裝)

851.486　　　　　　　　　　　　　　102010587

讀者回函卡

感謝您購買本書，為提升服務品質，請填妥以下資料，將讀者回函卡直接寄回或傳真本公司，收到您的寶貴意見後，我們會收藏記錄及檢討，謝謝！如您需要了解本公司最新出版書目、購書優惠或企劃活動，歡迎您上網查詢或下載相關資料：http:// www.showwe.com.tw

您購買的書名：＿＿＿＿＿＿＿＿＿＿＿＿＿＿＿＿＿＿＿＿＿

出生日期：＿＿＿＿＿年＿＿＿＿＿月＿＿＿＿＿日

學歷：□高中 (含) 以下　　□大專　　□研究所 (含) 以上

職業：□製造業　□金融業　□資訊業　□軍警　□傳播業　□自由業
　　　□服務業　□公務員　□教職　　□學生　□家管　□其它＿＿＿

購書地點：□網路書店　□實體書店　□書展　□郵購　□贈閱　□其他

您從何得知本書的消息？

　　□網路書店　□實體書店　□網路搜尋　□電子報　□書訊　□雜誌
　　□傳播媒體　□親友推薦　□網站推薦　□部落格　□其他＿＿＿＿＿

您對本書的評價：（請填代號　1.非常滿意　2.滿意　3.尚可　4.再改進）

　　封面設計＿＿＿　版面編排＿＿＿　內容＿＿＿　文／譯筆＿＿＿　價格＿＿＿

讀完書後您覺得：

　　□很有收穫　□有收穫　□收穫不多　□沒收穫

對我們的建議：＿＿＿＿＿＿＿＿＿＿＿＿＿＿＿＿＿＿＿＿＿

＿＿＿＿＿＿＿＿＿＿＿＿＿＿＿＿＿＿＿＿＿＿＿＿＿＿＿＿＿

＿＿＿＿＿＿＿＿＿＿＿＿＿＿＿＿＿＿＿＿＿＿＿＿＿＿＿＿＿

＿＿＿＿＿＿＿＿＿＿＿＿＿＿＿＿＿＿＿＿＿＿＿＿＿＿＿＿＿

11466
台北市內湖區瑞光路 76 巷 65 號 1 樓
秀威資訊科技股份有限公司　　　收
BOD 數位出版事業部

....

（請沿線對折寄回，謝謝！）

姓　　名：＿＿＿＿＿＿＿＿＿　年齡：＿＿＿＿　性別：□女　□男

郵遞區號：□□□□□

地　　址：＿＿＿＿＿＿＿＿＿＿＿＿＿＿＿＿＿＿＿＿＿＿

聯絡電話：(日)＿＿＿＿＿＿＿＿＿＿　(夜)＿＿＿＿＿＿＿＿＿＿

E-mail：＿＿＿＿＿＿＿＿＿＿＿＿＿＿＿＿＿＿＿＿